Casey at the Bat

VISIONS IN POETRY

Ernest L. Thayer

CASEY AT THE BAT

WITH ILLUSTRATIONS BY
JOE MORSE

KCP POETRY
AN IMPRINT OF KIDS CAN PRESS

AND NOW THE LEATHER-COVERED SPHERE CAME **HURTLING** THROUGH THE AIR,

AND **CASEY** STOOD A-WATCHING IT IN HAUGHTY GRANDEUR THERE.

"THAT AIN'T MY STYLE," SAID CASEY.

CLOSE BY THE STURDY BATSMAN THE BALL **UNHEEDED** SPED —

WITH A SMILE OF CHRISTIAN CHARITY
    GREAT CASEY'S VISAGE SHONE;
HE STILLED THE RISING TUMULT;
    HE BADE THE GAME GO ON;
HE SIGNALED TO THE PITCHER,
    AND ONCE MORE THE DUN SPHERE FLEW;
BUT CASEY STILL IGNORED IT,

BUT THERE IS NO JOY IN MUDVILLE —
MIGHTY CASEY HAS **STRUCK OUT.**

Ernest L. Thayer

American writer and poet Ernest Lawrence Thayer (1863–1940) is perhaps best known today as the author of "Casey at the Bat." After graduating from Harvard in 1885, where he was the editor of the *Harvard Lampoon*, Thayer began working as a humor columnist for the *San Francisco Examiner*. "Casey at the Bat: A Ballad of the Republic, Sung in the Year 1888" appeared in the June 3, 1888, issue under Thayer's byline, "Phin." But it took a recitation of the poem later that year by actor De Wolf Hopper, at a show for the New York Giants and the Chicago White Stockings, for it to gain notoriety. Hopper didn't discover who wrote the ballad until Thayer attended one of his by-then legendary performances of "Casey" about five years later and granted the actor rights to recite the poem without paying any royalties. It was well into the 1900s, however, before Thayer was widely accepted as the true author. Thayer's reluctance to assert his claim to "Casey" seems to have something to do with the fact that he considered it one of his mediocre works, remarking, "Its persistent vogue is simply unaccountable, and it would be hard to say, all things considered, if it has given me more pleasure than annoyance."

Despite its creator's modest opinion, "Casey" remains one of the most treasured poems in the English language. It is a poem that is as much a part of baseball as hot dogs, the national anthem and the seventh-inning stretch. Yet its appeal is not limited to enthusiasts of the sport or of poetry. "Casey" has been recited in theatres, ballparks and classrooms, and has inspired parodies, sequels, books, films, operas, paintings, cartoons and television shows. Thayer's poem is a part of the very fabric of American culture, a status that was confirmed in 1996 when the United States Postal Service issued a Casey stamp as part of a series saluting American folk heroes. Although "the outlook wasn't brilliant for the Mudville nine that day," the future of Thayer's fictional slugger proved to be very bright indeed; Mighty Casey struck out that fateful day in Mudville, but he has been immortalized in verse, bringing joy to generations of fans.

Joe Morse

Joe Morse's vision of "Casey at the Bat" marks a bold departure from the many nostalgically illustrated editions of the poem. Reinventing this American classic for a new generation, Morse portrays the cool, swaggering Casey (a.k.a. KC) and his Mudville 9 as a group of multiracial inner-city kids playing ball in an urban jungle of concrete buildings, chain-link fences and graffiti-covered walls. It is a particularly relevant approach in an era where kids dream of escaping their present-day realities by following in the footsteps of the sports figures they idolize.

Although Morse has put a contemporary spin on "Casey," his powerful depiction of the intensity, emotion and drama of the verse and of baseball itself stays true to the poem's spirit. Morse's images paint a compelling portrait of human nature, particularly the psychology of the hero and the crowd. Indeed, this interpretation of "Casey" transforms Thayer's caricatures into flesh-and-blood people with real hopes and dreams — and real vulnerability. Here, the muscular, towering figure of Mighty Casey is much more than an arrogant showman. He is someone who is ultimately confined by the batting cage and the concrete boxes of his surroundings, deserted by even his most ardent fans. Morse explores the idea of the hero in the context of modern culture, where the line between celebrity and heroism is sadly blurred. With Morse's singular vision and striking images, this hard-hitting edition of "Casey" is clearly a grand slam.

Joe Morse paints outside year round in headphones, a baseball cap and, due to the toxicity of his materials, a gas mask. His art is exhibited in numerous private and public collections in North America and has won many international honors, such as awards from the New York Society of Illustrators, *Communication Arts* and *American Illustration*. His impressive list of commercial clients includes Nike, *The New Yorker*, *Rolling Stone* and Universal Pictures. Director of the Degree Program in Illustration at Sheridan Institute, Morse lives in Toronto, Ontario, with his wife, artist Lorraine Tuson, and their two children.

To Lorraine, for making each of these pictures live,
and to my mother, Andrea, who has inspired me
with her love of all that life has to bring — J.M.

The illustrations for this book were
rendered in oil and acrylic on paper.

The text was set in

DEVICE and Impact

KCP Poetry is an imprint of Kids Can Press

First paperback edition 2010

Illustrations © 2006 Joe Morse

Kids Can Press acknowledges the financial support of the Government of
Ontario, through the Ontario Media Development Corporation's Ontario Book
Initiative; the Ontario Arts Council; the Canada Council for the Arts; and the
Government of Canada, through the BPIDP, for our publishing activity.

Published in Canada by
Kids Can Press Ltd.
29 Birch Avenue
Toronto, ON M4V 1E2

Published in the U.S. by
Kids Can Press Ltd.
2250 Military Road
Tonawanda, NY 14150

www.kidscanpress.com

Edited by Tara Walker
Designed by Karen Powers
Printed and bound in China

The hardcover edition of this book is smyth sewn casebound.
The paperback edition of this book is limp sewn with a drawn-on cover.

CM 06 0 9 8 7 6 5 4 3 2 1
CM PA 10 0 9 8 7 6 5 4 3 2 1

Library and Archives Canada Cataloguing in Publication

Thayer, Ernest Lawrence, 1863–1940
Casey at the bat / Ernest L. Thayer ; with illustrations by Joe Morse.

(Visions in poetry)

ISBN 978-1-55337-827-3 (bound)   ISBN 978-1-55453-458-6 (pbk.)

1. Children's poetry, American. I. Morse, Joe, 1960–
II. Title. III. Series: Visions in poetry

PS3014.T3C38 2010   j811'.52   C2009-903620-7

Kids Can Press is a *Corus* Entertainment company